HOW TO REMOVE
MOVIE PROJECTOR FROM BOOK

Cut off plastic tie and discard. Hold on to
handle and lift projector straight out of base.
To store projector, simply snap back into the base.

HOW TO USE THIS PROJECTOR

- Pick a clear space on a light-colored wall or ceiling three to five feet away.
- The biggest image can be seen when the projector is five feet from the wall or ceiling.
- Use Disk 1 to begin. Change disks as indicated in the story.
- Slide the picture disk into the slot in the top of the projector as shown.
- Turn the disk to the right as you read through the story. The numbers next to the text correspond to the numbers on the projected images. Use the focusing ring to focus the pictures.

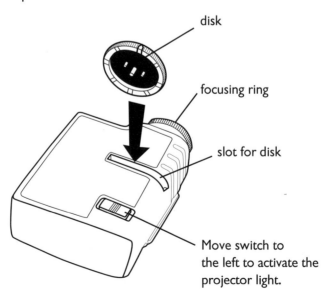

disk

focusing ring

slot for disk

Move switch to
the left to activate the
projector light.

nickelodeon™

PUPS SAVE THE PENGUINS

adapted by MacKenzie Buckley

studio **fun**

A READER'S DIGEST COMPANY

White Plains, New York • Montréal, Québec • Bath, United Kingdom

It was a beautiful day in Adventure Bay when Ryder assembled the PAW Patrol pups at the Lookout.

"Something fishy is happening on Cap'n Turbot's boat," Ryder told the pups. "We need to find out who is swiping his seafood.

"Chase, we need your detective skills and spy gear," he said.

Disk 1

1

"Zuma, we need you, too!" said Ryder.

"Let's dive in!" said Zuma.

"PAW Patrol is on a roll!" said Ryder as the team zoomed off in their vehicles.

When they reached the bay, Ryder's ATV and Zuma's vehicle transformed into hovercrafts. They sped across the water to reach Cap'n Turbot's boat, *The Flounder.*

Ryder and Zuma climbed on board. Chase made a surprise, high-impact entrance!

"Thanks for coming so quickly," Cap'n Turbot said. "So, how do we snare these seafood-snatching suspects?"

Zuma pushed a bucket of fish-flavored pup treats forward. "Let's set a trap," he suggested. "We can use these treats as bait."

Ryder noticed that one treat was already missing! "Somebody took one," he said. "Right from under our noses!"

Chase began to sniff around the bucket for clues.

"I'm smelling something I've never smelled before!" said Chase. He followed his nose—and the scent—all over the ship, even going up the sides of the walls.

In the meantime, Ryder and Zuma took a treat and explored the water surrounding the ship. (4) Someone grabbed the treat out of Ryder's hand without him seeing a thing!

That night, Chase put on his night goggles to help him track the thieves.

"Aha!" he cried. "Footprints!"

Chase followed the footprints to a room below deck. He found something! But it wasn't the fish stealers.

Disk 2

①

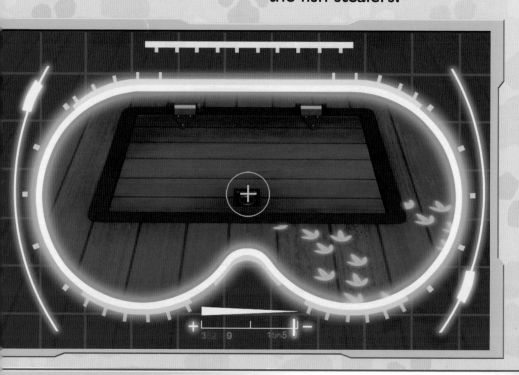

Ryder suggested they put the bucket of fish-flavored treats out on deck again.

"Spy Chase is on the case!" said Chase, as he positioned himself to watch the bucket.

Suddenly, a penguin appeared to steal the snack!

"Zip line!" Chase commanded.

2

The penguin ducked out of Chase's grasp.

"Look, there's more than one!" Zuma cried.

He and Chase tried to stop them, but the penguins slipped away.

"Sorry, Cap'n Turbot," said Chase.

"The stolen seafood is the least of our problems," said Cap'n Turbot. "It's too warm for the penguins to live in Adventure Bay. We need to get them back to their cold homes."

"They must have ridden that iceberg up here," said Ryder, pointing to a huge floating mountain of solid ice. "Maybe they can ride it home if we can get them on it."

"But how can we lure them onto it?" asked Chase. "We're all out of fish."

"What about my squid jerky? Those pilfering penguins won't be able to resist," said Cap'n Turbot.

"That stuff stinks," said Chase.

"Yes it does," Cap'n Turbot agreed proudly.

"I'll take the jerky to the iceberg," said Zuma.

It worked! In no time the penguins were on the iceberg, ready to snack some more.

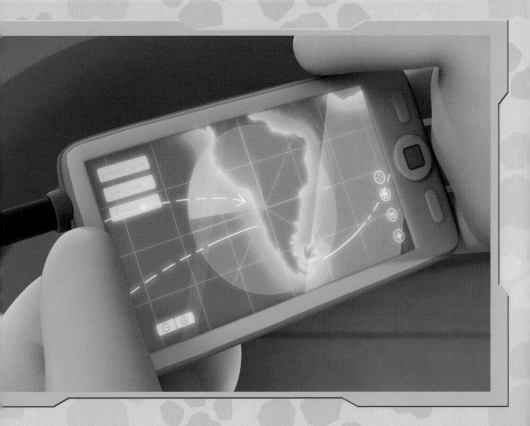

Now the PAW Patrol had to get the iceberg back to colder waters before it melted. Cap'n Turbot checked his lighthouse log to find a frigate headed far enough south.

"Fantastic!" he cried. "A frozen fish-carrying frigate is headed to the tip of South America!"

"Time to move an iceberg!" Ryder said, excitedly. The PAW Patrol attached the iceberg to the frigate and watched it—and the penguins—sail away.

Cap'n Turbot turned to Ryder and Chase. "Thanks for helping the penguins hitch a ride back to colder waters," he said.

(4) "No job is too big, no pup is too small!" replied Ryder.

BATTERY INFORMATION

To remove or insert replaceable batteries, remove the safety screw from battery compartment door. Lift and remove door. Take out and safely dispose of old batteries. Follow polarity diagram inside battery compartment to insert three new batteries of any of the following types: AG13 or equivalent. Alkaline batteries are recommended. Put battery compartment door back and secure safety screw. Do not use excess force or an improper type or size screwdriver.

GENERAL SAFETY AND CARE

- Non-rechargeable batteries are not to be recharged.
- Different types of batteries or new and used batteries are not to be mixed.
- Batteries are to be inserted with the correct polarity.
- Exhausted batteries are to be removed from the toy.
- The supply terminals are not to be short-circuited.
- Do not mix old and new batteries.
- Do not mix alkaline, standard (carbon-zinc), or rechargeable (nickel-cadmium) batteries.
- Prevent the book and unit from getting wet and avoid exposure to excessively hot or cold temperatures.
- Rechargeable batteries are only to be charged under adult supervision.
- Rechargeable batteries are to be removed from the toy before being charged.
- Remove batteries when not in use or discharged.

CAUTION

To ensure proper safety and operation, battery replacement must always be done by an adult. Never let a child use this product unless battery door is secure. Batteries are small objects and could be ingested. Keep all batteries away from small children and immediately dispose of any used batteries safely. Projector is not a viewer. Do not look into the lens when light is on.

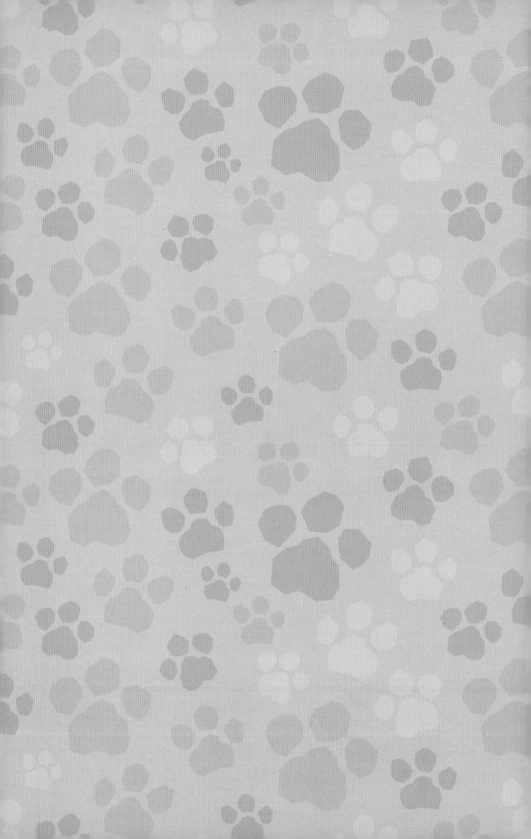